DUN

WITHDRAWN

Nothing was too good for Little Miss Splendid.

She lived in a huge house surrounded by large gardens.

She slept in an enormous bed with silk sheets and silk pillowcases.

She bathed in a gold bath.

And she dined off silver plates.

Oh, she was splendid!

At least, she thought so.

Little Miss Splendid thought a lot of herself.

In fact, she thought about little else!

One day, while taking a stroll around her gardens, Little Miss Splendid came upon a small door in one of the walls.

She'd never noticed it before.

"I wonder what's through here?" she thought and, opening the door, she stepped through.

She found herself on a road.

Along came Mr Small, out for a short walk.

"Good morning," he remarked politely, raising his hat.

Little Miss Splendid stuck her nose even higher in the air, and walked past him as if he wasn't there.

"What a common little man," she thought to herself.

She came to a bus stop.

Mr Happy and Mr Daydream were waiting for a bus into town.

"Hello," grinned Mr Happy.

"Who are you?"

"I," she replied, "am Splendid!"

"Oh," said Mr Happy.

"Are you going to catch the bus?" asked Mr Daydream.

"Me?" she said.

"The bus?"

"Never!!"

"I," she went on, "have never ever in the whole of my life travelled on a bus!"

An expression of distaste crossed her face.

"You have to sit next to people on buses," she went on. "And that would never do!"

"Oh," said Mr Happy, and scratched his head.

He couldn't think of anything to say.

Miss Splendid walked off with her nose very high in the air.

Miss Splendid arrived in town.

She looked at herself in all the shop windows as she walked down the street.

"I must say," she thought to herself, "I do look absolutely splendid."

And then something caught her eye.

There, in the middle of the window of the hat shop, was a hat.

Not just a hat.

A hat and a half!

The most magnificent, sumptuous, desirable, gorgeous, spectacular, amazing, splendid hat you've ever seen.

Miss Splendid marched into the shop.

She snapped her fingers, and a saleslady hurried to her side.

"Good morning Madam," the saleslady said.

Miss Splendid ignored her.

"Can I help you?"

"I," announced Miss Splendid, "wish to try on the hat in the window!"

Miss Splendid looked at herself in the mirror.

"Magnificent," she breathed.

"I look absolutely magnificent!"

"I'll take it," she announced.

"But don't you want to know how much it costs?" asked the saleslady.

"Costs?" queried Miss Splendid loftily.

"I never discuss money matters!"

"Send me the bill!"

And she marched out of the shop.

Little Miss Splendid stood on the pavement, and held up her hand.

"Taxi!" she announced in a loud important voice.

A taxi stopped.

"Take me home," she ordered, and went to get in, but of course she couldn't.

Her new hat was much too large to fit through the taxi door.

"Driver," she said. "You should purchase yourself a larger taxi!"

"In the meantime," she went on, "I shall walk!"

The taxi driver grinned.

Little Miss Splendid walked along.

"Perhaps it's better to walk," she thought
to herself.

"So that everyone has the chance to admire
my magnificent new hat."

But then it happened.

It started to rain!

And the trouble was, the more it started to rain, the more it rained.

And the trouble was, the more it rained, the more Miss Splendid got wet.

And the trouble was, the wetter she got, the wetter her hat got.

What a sorry sight!

Don't you agree?

The bus, on its return journey from town, passed her.

Mr Happy and Mr Daydream, on their way home and sitting in the dry, looked out of the window.

"I say," remarked Mr Happy, looking out at the bedraggled figure trudging along in the wet. "What a splendid sight!"

Mr Daydream giggled.

"Splendid," he agreed.

Miss Splendid, looking anything but splendid, arrived home.

However, after a hot bath in her gold bath, and after a boiled egg in a gold egg cup, eaten with a silver spoon, she felt much better.

In fact, later on, she spent an extremely pleasant evening looking at...

Well.

What do you think she spent all evening looking at?

No!

Not television.

Herself!

In the mirror!

Fantastic offers for Little Miss fans!

Collect all your Mr. Men or Little Miss books in these superb durable collectors' cases!

Only £5.99 inc. postage and packing, these wipe-clean, hard-wearing cases will give all your Mr. Men or Little Miss books a beautiful new home!

Keep track of your collection with this giant-sized double-sided Mr. Men and Little Miss Collectors' poster.

Collect 6 tokens and we will send you a brilliant giant-sized double-sided collectors' poster! Simply tape a £1 coin to cover postage and packaging in the space provided and fill out the form overleaf.

STICK £1 COIN HERE (for poster only)

Only need a few Little Miss or Mr. Men to complete your set? You can order any of the titles on the back of the books from our Mr. Men order line on 0870 787 1724. Orders should be delivered between 5 and 7 working days.

— TO BE COMPLETED BY AN ADULT —

To apply for any of these great offers, ask an adult to complete the details below and send this whole page with the appropriate payment and tokens, to: MR. MEN CLASSIC OFFER, PO BOX 715, HORSHAM RH12 5WG

☐ Please send me a giant-sized double-sided collectors' poster.

AND ☐ I enclose 6 tokens and have taped a £1 coin to the other side of this page.

☐ Please send me ☐ Mr. Men Library case(s) and/or ☐ Little Miss library case(s) at £5.99 each inc P&P

☐ I enclose a cheque/postal order payable to Egmont UK Limited for £...................

OR ☐ Please debit my MasterCard / Visa / Maestro / Delta account (delete as appropriate) for £...................

Card no. ☐☐☐☐ ☐☐☐☐ ☐☐☐☐ ☐☐☐☐ ☐☐☐☐   Security code ☐☐☐

Issue no. (if available) ☐   Start Date ☐☐/☐☐/☐☐   Expiry Date ☐☐/☐☐/☐☐

Fan's name: Date of birth:

Address:

           Postcode:

Name of parent / guardian:

Email for parent / guardian:

Signature of parent / guardian:

Please allow 28 days for delivery. Offer is only available while stocks last. We reserve the right to change the terms of this offer at any time and we offer a 14 day money back guarantee. This does not affect your statutory rights. Offers apply to UK only.

☐ We may occasionally wish to send you information about other Egmont children's books. If you would rather we didn't, please tick this box.

Ref: LIM 001